Project Mc²

THE **Pretty Brilliant**

EXPERIMENT BOOK

BY JADE HEMSWORTH

EXPERIMENTS PROVIDED BY DRS. MARGUERITE AND ZOLTÁN L. BENKŐ

【Imprint】
MAKE YOUR MARK

NEW YORK

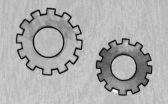

[Imprint]
MAKE YOUR MARK

A part of Macmillan Children's Publishing Group and Macmillan Publishing Group, LLC.

PROJECT MC2: THE PRETTY BRILLIANT EXPERIMENT BOOK. Copyright © 2017 by MGA, LLC.
All rights reserved. Printed in China by Toppan Leefung Printing Ltd., Dongguan City, Guangdong Province.
For information, address Imprint, 175 Fifth Avenue, New York, N.Y. 10010.

Library of Congress Cataloging-in-Publication Data is available.

ISBN 978-1-250-10369-7 (paperback) / ISBN 978-1-250-10368-0 (ebook)

Our books may be purchased in bulk for promotional, educational, or business use. Please contact
your local bookseller or the Macmillan Corporate and Premium Sales Department
at (800) 221-7945 ext. 5442 or by e-mail at MacmillanSpecialMarkets@macmillan.com.

Book design by Kayleigh McCann

Imprint logo designed by Amanda Spielman

First Edition—2017

1 3 5 7 9 10 8 6 4 2

mackids.com

S.L.N.B.
(Steal Looks, Not Books.)

CONTENTS:

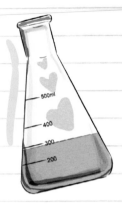

© MGA

INTRODUCTION: THE TIME TRAP!

The NOV8 team were secret agents and friends—best friends, maybe—since nothing made people bond like being held hostage together. They could barely see each other in the dim room. It couldn't have been more than twelve feet wide by twelve feet long, with a low ceiling and just one tiny window that hardly let in any light. Time was running out, and they needed to break free before the floor gave out beneath them and they were dropped into a pit of hungry piranhas below.

Camryn Coyle, NOV8's construction queen, tugged against the rope. It was tied around her wrists, tethering her to the chair. "It's too tight," she said. "I can't move."

"Neither can I," tech guru Bryden Bandweth said.

"We're running out of time," McKeyla McAlister, the team leader, added.

A voice sounded from a speaker on the wall. "One minute."

"I can't believe we're going to be dropped into a pit of hungry piranhas!" Adrienne Attoms, a culinary chemist,

tried to turn around to look at her friends. She could only catch the tiniest glimpse of Camryn. All four of their chairs were tied together, back to back.

"I hate piranhas!" Camryn said, wincing. "They're like goldfish with teeth."

"Sharks would've been better," Bryden said. "One bite and it would all be over."

McKeyla looked up at the small window below the ceiling. A thin stream of light cut across the floor. She thought of the different inventions she and her NOV8 team had come up with in the past weeks, while training for their next mission. Were there any that could save them now?

"Hold on, guys, I have an idea," McKeyla said. "Adri, do you have your compact?"

Adrienne frowned. "Why, am I shiny?"

"A little, but that's not why I need it," McKeyla said. "Bry, if you can reach into Adri's pocket, then you can hand it to me, then I can hand it to Cam."

"Oh . . . so she's the shiny one," Adrienne said, obviously relieved. "I was going to say something but I didn't think now was the time."

Bryden carefully reached into Adrienne's back pocket, letting the compact slip into her hand. She passed it to McKeyla, who passed it to Camryn, who flipped it open. Adrienne had designed the compact weeks ago. After their last mission, she'd fastened a magnifying glass inside it so it could perfect her complexion *and* help them if they were in a tough situation. The girls were always coming up with new inventions and trying to improve the old ones to prepare for whatever they had to face next.

"I see where you're going," Camryn said, angling the magnifying glass so it caught the stream of light. "All I have to do is move it so that all the solar radiation hitting the lens focuses to a tiny point, raising the temperature of that spot enough for a chemical reaction to occur."

The voice boomed through the speaker: "Thirty seconds."

Camryn angled the lens back and forth, aiming the beam of light at the rope tying McKeyla's hands. The beam generated so much solar energy that a tiny wisp of smoke streamed up from it as it began to burn.

"It's working!" Camryn smiled.

In just a few seconds, the rope snapped, freeing McKeyla. She stood and untied the rest of the girls. "Oh yeah, oh yeah!" the girls sang. "We're free. We're unstoppable!"

"And still trapped in here!" McKeyla said. She felt around the room, but it was so dark she could barely see anything. She couldn't even find the door.

"My nail polish!" Adrienne said, pulling the tiny bottle from her spy bag. She twisted the top and it turned into a tiny flashlight. She accidentally shined it in McKeyla's eyes.

"Temporarily blinded!" McKeyla winced. "Not good!"

"Ten seconds," the voice boomed from the loudspeaker.

Adrienne's light caught what looked like a crack in the wall. When she moved in, studying it closely, she could see two hinges camouflaged by paint. "This is it! The way out!"

Camryn wiggled her hand in her pocket and pulled out a rectangular object that unfolded to become a tiny screwdriver. She wedged it in the crack in the wall, trying to find the exact place where the lock mechanism met the frame. She leaned all her weight into it. In an instant, the door came free. The girls ran out just as the voice on the speaker boomed again: "Time's up!"

"We did it, we're free! Go, us! Go, us!" the girls all sang, dancing with one another.

"Well done, girls," the Quail said from a computer monitor on the wall. She looked down at them and smiled. "Another impressive training session. You're all showing great progress."

Even though it had felt really real, there was no pit of hungry piranhas waiting to devour the girls. McKeyla's lab was bright and cheery compared to the dark training room where they'd just been trapped. They'd been running drills like this for weeks, preparing for their next mission. The last time they'd managed to burn through the ropes, but they hadn't found the secret door in the wall. The Quail was right—they definitely were making progress.

"Keep up the good work," the Quail said. She was the NOV8 chief intelligence agent, and gave them missions and told McKeyla what to do (since she was McKeyla's mom, too). "I'll be in touch soon with the next mission."

With that, her screen shut off. Adrienne, Bryden, and Camryn all turned to McKeyla.

"How soon?" Bryden asked. "What's a NOV8 agent without a NOV8 mission?"

"I don't know," McKeyla said. "But I've heard murmurings that there's a new villain in Maywood Glen. We can never be too prepared."

The girls nodded, slowly drifting back to their places in the lab. Camryn huddled over her hoverboard. Adrienne was working on a new recipe for gummies, and Bryden was working on the circuitry within her light-up earrings. As McKeyla sat down at her workbench, she looked at her friends. Whoever this villain was, whatever he or she wanted . . . NOV8 would be ready.

Section One:
McKeyla McAlister

I'M **Smart.** get over it!™

It's hard to work in candlelight. That was pretty much my only choice, though. All of Maywood Glen is dark. A mysterious villain has shut down our entire power grid, so we're in the middle of a massive blackout. My team and I are going to track him down, but first I need to put a few supplies together. We have to be ready to move as soon as we find his location.

We're obviously not going to walk around Maywood Glen with candles or torches, like we just stepped out of the Middle Ages or something. And we can't be carrying around big flashlights during a mission. We need something that won't look odd to the random person who sees it in our backpack or locker. I've been on enough missions to know the situation can change at any moment, so you want to make sure your supplies are as covert as you are. Those supplies shouldn't scream, *Look at me! I'm part of a secret spy organization that has sleeper cells in every country all over the world!*

That's why I designed the glitter lightbulbs. Okay, so maybe the glitter was Adrienne's idea (she says everything is better with glitter and I'm starting to think she's right). The supplies were simple—glycerin, water, lightbulbs, and a few portable battery packs. There were certainly enough lightbulbs in my house just sitting there in lamps that wouldn't turn on. I figured I'd put those babies to good use.

I still had to make the last one. I filled the bulb with glitter, water, and glycerin, which helped magnify the light. Then I carefully put the bottom of the lightbulb back on, using a super-strong superglue Adrienne had made especially for me.

After I finished, I hooked up the lightbulb to a portable battery pack! Ta-da! A flashlight that was smaller and more efficient than the ones you buy at stores and perfectly disguised as a household lightbulb. I was going to start working on my next invention, a headband that had lights across the front of it, but then my phone buzzed.

BRY: T.A.D.Q.M.I.T.G.I.F.M.

I'd been friends with Bryden for months, but it still wasn't easy to figure out her long, complicated acronyms. I stared at it for a good five minutes before realizing what she meant. Things Are Developing Quickly. Meet In The Garage In Five Minutes. So . . . basically: Meet us in the garage *now*!

I collected the glitter lightbulbs and hurried out the door toward the garage. I could see they'd already turned on the backup generator. There was a thin stream of light peeking out from under the door.

I powered on my lightbulb, letting it lead the way. The rest of my neighborhood was completely dark, with the exception of a few flickering candles in the windows. I thought of Miss Roberta, an elderly woman who lived in the house across the way. She was totally alone. How would she get around her house when it was pitch-black outside?

We had to find who cut the power, and fast. All of Maywood Glen was depending on us.

These last few months I've gotten obsessed with all the different inventions I can use on my missions. Check out some of my favorite experiments you can do on your own at home!

McKeyla's Experiments

- The Sands of Time

- DNA

- Möbius Magic

- Catching the Moon

- Jane and the Beanstalk

- A Question of Balance

- Chromatography: Race to the Top

THE
SANDS OF TIME

THIS EXPERIMENT REQUIRES ADULT ASSISTANCE.

Got a minute? Let's make an hourglass.

MATERIALS

- ✖ 2 clear plastic water bottles, 250–500 milliliters (mL) or 8–20 fluid ounces (fl oz), with caps
- ✖ roll of masking tape
- ✖ drill
- ✖ sheet of paper
- ✖ 100 mL or 7 tablespoons (tbsp) of dry sand
- ✖ watch

ADULTS ONLY FOR THIS STEP!

1 Tape the bottle caps tightly together, top to top. Ask an adult to drill a 5 millimeter (mm) or ¼ inch (in) hole through the middle and smooth away any burrs.

2 Fold a sturdy piece of paper and place 100 mL (7 tbsp) of sand in the crease. Tip all the sand into one bottle and screw both bottles into the caps. Turn your hourglass so that the sand in the top bottle flows into the lower one.

3 Use the watch to determine how long it takes for the sand to pass from one bottle to the other.

4 Try to adjust your hourglass by adding or removing sand so that it runs for exactly 30 seconds.

OBSERVATIONS AND RESULTS

You have just made an hourglass by trial and error. Making a small change and observing the result, then making a new change based on the observation is a common technique used by scientists and inventors.

FOR THE RECORD

You can measure time with the help of gravity. Trial and error helps you figure out things and improve inventions. Never give up!

TEST IT YOURSELF

How would you use your new upcycled hourglass to keep track of time all day long, the way your watch does? Can you think of a better way to keep track of time, without electricity?

A.D.I.S.N. SAYS:

Sure, it's easy for *you* to tell time—all you have to do is look at your phone or check out the watch strapped to your wrist. But in ancient times, making a reliable time-telling device required A LOT of experimentation. Sand, water, and oil were used at first, but now we use metal, plastic, and quartz crystals to tell time accurately. You don't want to be late to your quiz, do you? (Or maybe you *do*. . . .)

DNA

The ultimate secret code for the ultimate secret agent.

MATERIALS

- ✖ 120 mL or 4 fl oz of 91% rubbing alcohol
- ✖ 10 mL or 2 teaspoons (tsp) of liquid dish soap
- ✖ 5 mL or 1 tsp of salt
- ✖ 100 mL or 3 fl oz of water
- ✖ 5–6 ripe strawberries
- ✖ sealable plastic bag, sandwich size or bigger
- ✖ coffee filter
- ✖ drinking glass
- ✖ toothpick

1. Cool rubbing alcohol ahead of time by placing the bottle in freezer.

2. Dissolve 10 mL (2 tsp) of liquid dish soap and 5 mL (1 tsp) of salt in 100 mL (3 fl oz) of water.

3. Place strawberries in plastic bag and seal. Mash up fruit to a smooth paste. Add about half the solution you prepared to the bag and knead gently. Allow to stand 20 to 30 minutes.

4. Tuck coffee filter into glass and fold edge out over rim. While holding filter paper in place, pour fruit-and-solution mixture on top and allow liquid to run through. Remove filter.

5. Gently pour an equal amount of chilled rubbing alcohol down the inside wall of the glass so that it forms a layer on top of the solution. Start off with a tablespoon at a time.

6. A fine cotton-like mass will form in the upper layer. Use a toothpick to lift out some of this slimy substance to take a closer look.

Although you mashed up the strawberries, the DNA (deoxyribonucleic acid) molecules were still inside the cells. Adding dish soap broke down the cell walls, releasing the DNA into the water solution. Adding the rubbing alcohol allowed the DNA to come out of the solution so that you could see it.

DNA molecules are like exceedingly long double-stranded necklaces that are made up of only four kinds of beads. The bead patterns are a code that provides instructions on how to make every part of a cell. In fact, the DNA in each cell provides enough information to make an entire organism! It does this by telling the cells how to assemble life's building blocks—amino acids—into proteins. Proteins provide most of the structure of living cells and control many of the processes that occur in them.

A strand of your longest DNA stretched out would be about 85 mm long, or just under 3.5 in, but if it were as thick as an ordinary piece of sewing thread, it would be over 10 kilometers or 6 miles long. That's more than the length of 100 football fields!

DNA can be extracted from cells. These molecules are very long but are made up of only four types of subunits. All the information needed to make a living organism is coded in these molecules.

TEST IT YOURSELF

We say that DNA is the "Code of Life," but how do you read the secret message? DNA simply shows the order in which to link amino acids together into proteins (see diagram, next page). You can think of the 4 beads in the necklace as letters. It turns out that in this code language all the words are exactly 3 letters long. There are only so many ways to combine 4 letters into 3-letter words, so the entire DNA code language is 64 words. You might think this isn't very many, but there are only 20 different amino acids these words need to represent. This could mean that most of the words aren't used in the code, but it could also mean something else. What would that be?

STRAND OF DNA

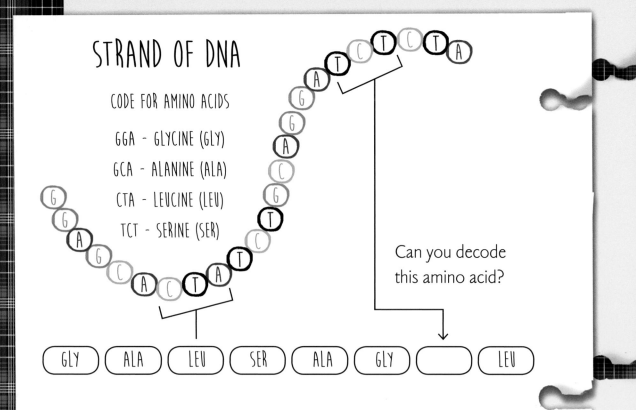

CODE FOR AMINO ACIDS

GGA – GLYCINE (GLY)

GCA – ALANINE (ALA)

CTA – LEUCINE (LEU)

TCT – SERINE (SER)

Can you decode this amino acid?

| GLY | ALA | LEU | SER | ALA | GLY | | LEU |

A.D.I.S.N. SAYS:

There may be only 64 words in the DNA code, but the sentences are extremely long. The 20 building blocks can be strung together in trillions and trillions of different ways. If DNA defines all living organisms—from the smallest bacteria to the largest blue whales—it defines you, too. (And awesome things like talking-notebook best friends!)

MÖBIUS MAGIC <3

If you don't know Möbius, you're not in the loop.

PROCEDURE

1 Cut three strips of paper that are 5 centimeters (cm) or 2 inches (in) wide and at least 30 cm or 12 in long. Draw a straight line down the middle of each strip. On one side, label each end with the letter *A*. Turn the strip over, and label each end with the letter *B*.

A CUTE!

2 Form strip #1 into a loop, matching the *A* sides of the two ends. Secure with tape. Form strip #2 into a loop with *one* twist, matching the *A* side with the *B* side of the other end. Secure with tape. Form strip #3 into a loop with *two* twists, matching the *A* sides of the two ends. Secure with tape.

3 Take loop #1 and cut along the line all the way around. What did you get? Record the result.

4 Examine loop #2 carefully. Predict what you expect to happen if you cut along the line of this loop. Keep in mind the result from loop #1. Now go ahead and cut along the line all the way around. Record the result.

5 Study loop #3 closely. Predict what you expect to happen if you cut along the line of this loop. Keep in mind the result from loops #1 and #2. Now go ahead and cut along the line all the way around. Record the result.

I KNOW!

	PREDICTED RESULT	RESULT OBTAINED
LOOP #1		
LOOP #2		
LOOP #3		

RESULTS

Loop #2 is known as a Möbius strip and has special properties—it has only one side and one edge.

When you made a prediction based on what you knew or observed, you were forming a hypothesis. You then tested your hypothesis and did an experiment to find out if you were correct. This entire process is called the scientific method. Sometimes things turn out exactly how you expect, and that is good. Every now and then, however, you get a big surprise, something totally unexpected. And isn't that great, too?

FOR THE RECORD

The Möbius strip has special properties. Using the scientific method is a great way to make discoveries.

TEST IT YOURSELF

Mathematicians and physicists love the Möbius strip because it makes them think differently about space and dimensions. It helps them come up with new ways to understand our universe. What do you think would happen if you put a third twist in the loop?

A.D.I.S.N. SAYS:

Got a hunch? Use the scientific method to test it out! It's a logical, step-by-step procedure, and it's responsible for almost every major discovery and invention in the last 500 years. They say if you use the scientific method, you ARE a scientist!

CATCHING
THE MOON

It's just going through a phase.

MATERIALS

* hole punch
* 30 cm or 12 in diameter flexible plastic flowerpot, black inside
* golf ball and tee
* modeling clay
* bright flashlight

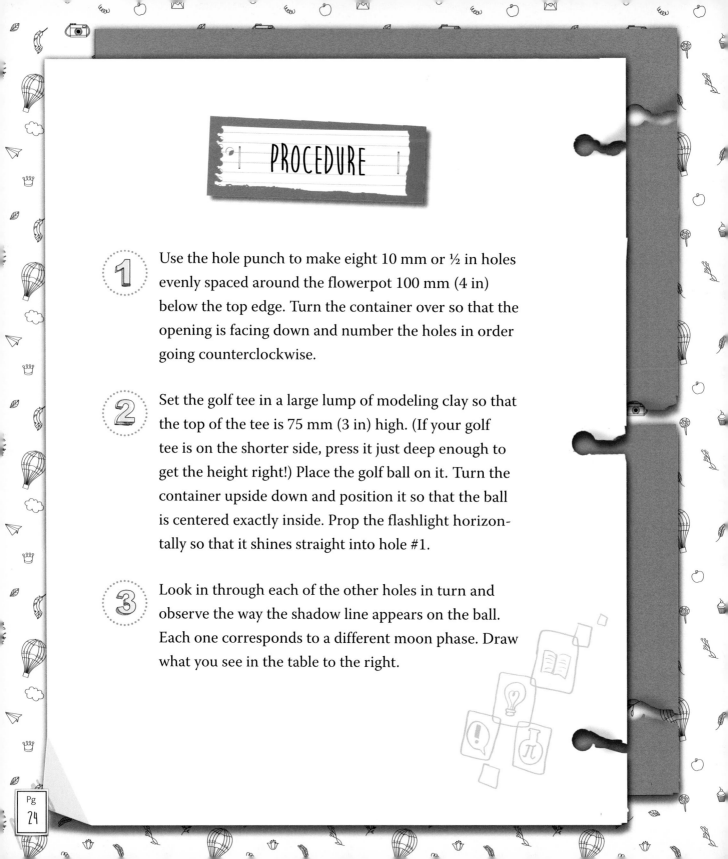

PROCEDURE

1 Use the hole punch to make eight 10 mm or ½ in holes evenly spaced around the flowerpot 100 mm (4 in) below the top edge. Turn the container over so that the opening is facing down and number the holes in order going counterclockwise.

2 Set the golf tee in a large lump of modeling clay so that the top of the tee is 75 mm (3 in) high. (If your golf tee is on the shorter side, press it just deep enough to get the height right!) Place the golf ball on it. Turn the container upside down and position it so that the ball is centered exactly inside. Prop the flashlight horizontally so that it shines straight into hole #1.

3 Look in through each of the other holes in turn and observe the way the shadow line appears on the ball. Each one corresponds to a different moon phase. Draw what you see in the table to the right.

OBSERVATIONS

1) FULL MOON	
2) WANING GIBBOUS	
3) THIRD QUARTER	
4) WANING CRESCENT	
5) NEW MOON	
6) WAXING CRESCENT	
7) FIRST QUARTER	
8) WAXING GIBBOUS	

RESULTS

The moon revolves around Earth once every 29½ days. The sun lights up one side of the moon completely, but what we see is only a portion of this depending on where the moon is compared to the sun and Earth. As the moon changes position, the shadow line shifts, making the moon look like it is shrinking (waning) or expanding (waxing). Once a cycle, the moon is completely lit up (full moon), and once a cycle, it is completely dark (new moon). Looking through each hole lets you see the phase of your golf ball "moon" at different points in the moon's journey around Earth.

Look at your diagrams. Can you come up with a rule that helps you tell whether the moon is waxing or waning on any given night?

FOR THE RECORD

Moon phases are a result of the changing angle at which we see the moon as it travels around Earth.

TEST IT YOURSELF

Imagine you could look through hole #1 from the perspective of the flashlight. What would the phase look like?

A.D.I.S.N. SAYS:

The laws of physics that govern the motion of the Earth and moon, as far as we can tell, are the same in the entire universe. Understanding how Earth and the moon move with respect to each other helps us understand how planets and stars behave. You could say Earth and the moon are kind of like friends, like McKeyla and me!

JANE AND THE BEANSTALK

Once upon a time, our heroine climbed up to the sky. . . .

THIS EXPERIMENT REQUIRES ADULT ASSISTANCE.

MATERIALS

- colored pencils or crayons
- thin piece of cardboard
- scissors
- cotton ball and glue stick
- wire coat hanger and pliers (alternatively, a garden stake or ruler)
- potting soil and pebbles
- 15–20 cm or 6–8 in flowerpot or container
- 1–2 pole bean seeds (or other climbing variety)
- water and plant fertilizer
- masking tape

1. Draw and color a landscape and great, big sky on the cardboard. Cut it out. Pull the cotton ball into a long cloud shape and glue it along the top of the landscape.

ADULTS ONLY FOR THIS STEP!

2. Ask an adult to cut the coat hanger near the hook with pliers and straighten it. Use the pliers to make a loop in one end that just fits in the bottom of the flowerpot. Bend the loop under 90° so that when you put it in the pot the long end sticks straight up. (If you're using a garden stake or ruler, prop it up into the soil used for step 3.)

3. Add pebbles to the flowerpot and fill it with soil. Plant one to two bean seeds in the soil about 3 cm or 1 in deep. Water and fertilize the soil.

4. Tape your drawn and colored landscape to the wire, stake, or ruler, so that it appears to float in the air above the flowerpot. Place the planted bean in a sunny location and allow it to grow. Observe and make a note of any changes in the table on the next page. Help the plant find the wire when it gets big enough. Keep track of the height and draw any interesting features as they develop. Note when the beanstalk reaches the sky, and feel free to draw a heroine climbing up the tall beanstalk.

5. Make sure you water your bean plant regularly. If you prepare more than one flowerpot and landscape, you can put them in different locations and see which one is better for growing the plants. You can also do this with a friend and see whose beanstalk reaches the sky first.

DATE	HEIGHT (CM)	NOTES	ILLUSTRATION

RESULTS

We don't often notice it, but plants grow in a very organized step-by-step process. Biologists number these stages and have special names for all the different parts.

After a few days in the soil, the seed casing softens and a tiny early root (radicle) emerges. Almost at the same time, a sprout (hypocotyl) forms and starts to grow up and emerge from the soil. It brings with it an early leaf (cotyledon) from inside the seed, which is quite different from the true leaves that come after. Next you have a one-lobed (unifoliolate) leaf appear and then a series of three-lobed (trifoliolate) leaves as the plant grows taller.

Note that the growing point (meristem) is at the tip of the plant. If this growing part is removed, the plant will try to form new stems and you will get branching. Once your beanstalk reaches the sky, it would be a good idea to plant it in a garden. It will keep growing, flower, and eventually produce beans.

FOR THE RECORD

Plants grow in a very organized manner and go through several stages. The cotyledon is an early leaf that looks very different from the true leaves. The growing point of a plant is called the meristem.

TEST IT YOURSELF

Even though I love rainy days, we need the sunny ones, too! Plants grow by using energy from sunlight, which ends up being stored in all its parts. How many different ways does this stored plant energy get used?

A.D.I.S.N. SAYS:

Plants provide people with food, shelter, and energy. Scientists work hard at making these uses safe and practical. Crop and forest protection research, plant breeding, and biotechnology improve the lives of people around the world. I (ahem) am also improving lives. At least the lives of four particular NOV8 agents . . .

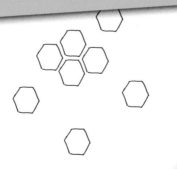

A QUESTION OF
BALANCE

Weight, weight, don't tell me.

MATERIALS

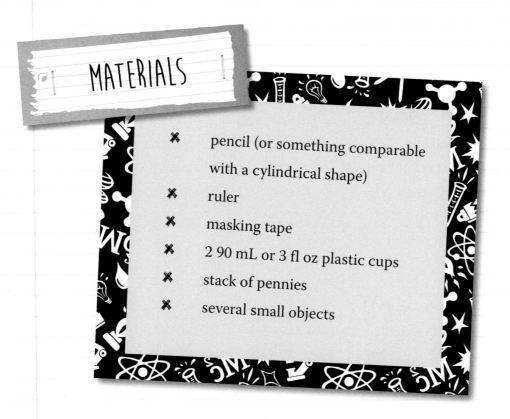

✖ pencil (or something comparable with a cylindrical shape)

✖ ruler

✖ masking tape

✖ 2 90 mL or 3 fl oz plastic cups

✖ stack of pennies

✖ several small objects

PROCEDURE

1 Clear off a workspace or table. Lay the pencil perpendicular to and exactly across the middle of the ruler—it doesn't matter which side—and secure it with a piece of masking tape. Flip the ruler over. Using loops of masking tape with the sticky side out, attach a small plastic cup to each end of the ruler. Make sure both ends are done exactly the same way. It looks like a seesaw but you just made a balance!

2 Pick up several small objects one at a time and notice how heavy they feel. Then arrange them in a row from lightest to heaviest.

3 Place a small object in one of the cups. Add pennies to the other cup until the weight pushes that end down and the ruler is level. Record the number of pennies in the table below.

4 Repeat the previous step for each of the other small objects. Did you get the order of lightest to heaviest correct?

5 You just weighed all the objects in terms of pennies. The penny was your standard unit of measure. A penny weighs 2.5 grams, so it is easy to convert the number of pennies into grams by multiplication. For example, if an object weighed 5 pennies, you would multiply 5 x 2.5 grams to get 12.5 grams.

OBJECT					
WEIGHT IN PENNIES					
WEIGHT IN GRAMS					

RESULTS

When you weigh an object, you are measuring how hard gravity is pulling on it. You can compare the amount of material in two objects with a balance, because the pull of gravity on the two ends is the same. The end of the balance goes down under the object that is made of more material.

If you use a standard unit of measure (like pennies or grams) you can compare several objects at once. Even though pennies aren't a common unit of measurement, they're convenient and easy to find! From there, it's easy to calculate the corresponding number of grams like you did in step 5. We do this because grams are a unit of measure used around the world—that way, scientists from all over can understand the results.

I KNOW!

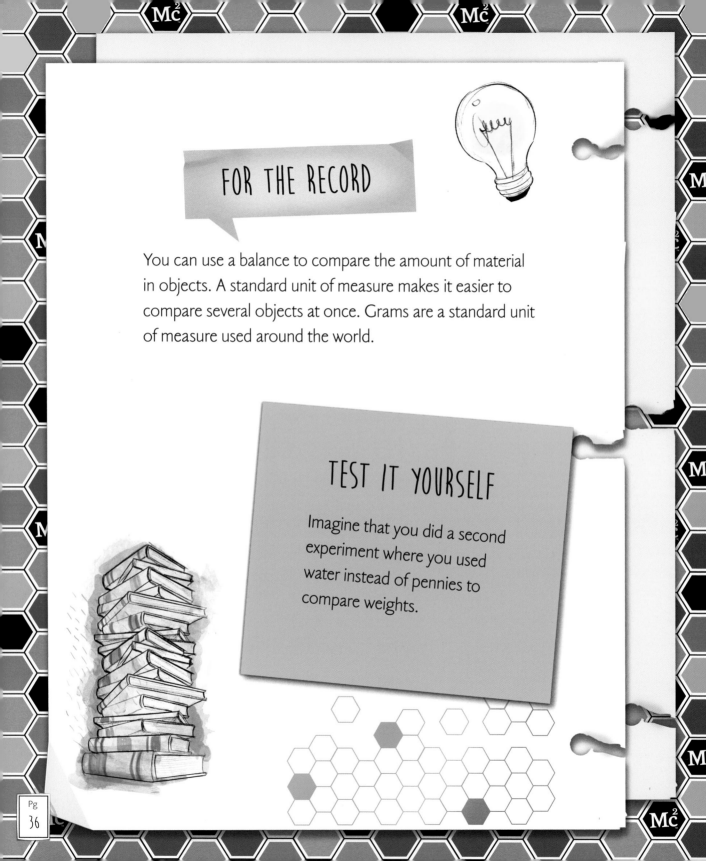

FOR THE RECORD

You can use a balance to compare the amount of material in objects. A standard unit of measure makes it easier to compare several objects at once. Grams are a standard unit of measure used around the world.

TEST IT YOURSELF

Imagine that you did a second experiment where you used water instead of pennies to compare weights.

A.D.I.S.N. SAYS:

You should always know how much material you need for a project. A rocket can only carry a certain amount into space, so it is a good idea to know how much it weighs.

Earth's surface gravity, or the gravitational acceleration experienced at its surface, changes depending on where you are on Earth. It is measured in meters per second squared (m/s^2). At the equator, Earth's surface gravity is 9.8 m/s^2. Compare that to Mars, where the surface gravity is 3.7 m/s^2, or the moon, which has a surface gravity of 1.6 m/s^2! The pennies would weigh a lot less on either of these planets, because there is less gravitational pull.

That's out of this world, right?

CHROMATOGRAPHY: RACE TO THE TOP

Color me pink . . . and blue and yellow and red.

THIS EXPERIMENT REQUIRES ADULT ASSISTANCE.

MATERIALS

- ✖ colored permanent markers
- ✖ white chalk sticks
- ✖ drill
- ✖ plastic water bottle caps
- ✖ 91% rubbing alcohol
- ✖ small dish

PROCEDURE

1 Using a colored permanent marker, draw a 1 mm wide (or very thin) ring around a chalk stick 2 cm (¾ in) from one end.

ADULTS ONLY FOR THIS STEP!

2 Ask an adult to use a drill to make a hole in the center of a water bottle cap just big enough so that it fits the chalk stick snugly and you can use it to stand the chalk stick on end.

3 Add rubbing alcohol to the small dish 1 cm (½ in) deep. Place the chalk stick in the holder with the ring end down and put it in the dish. The rubbing alcohol should slowly move up the chalk stick and carry the dyes in the ring along with it. It may take 30 minutes for the rubbing alcohol to get close to the top. (Don't get anything on your vintage T-shirt!)

4 Remove the chalk and let it dry. Repeat using a different colored marker or run several at a time. The dyes will separate into bands of color. Record your results in the table on the next page.

NUMBER	ORIGINAL MARKER COLOR	TOP BAND OF COLOR	SECOND BAND OF COLOR	THIRD BAND OF COLOR	NUMBER OF BANDS	BASELINE COLOR
1						
2						
3						
4						

RESULTS

In this experiment, the different dye molecules have a choice of being dissolved in the rubbing alcohol or staying on the chalk. Some molecules dissolve more easily in rubbing alcohol. Some molecules stick to chalk better. The rubbing alcohol, however, is moving (mobile phase), and anything dissolved in it moves along, too. The molecules that prefer the chalk (stationary phase) get left behind.

Separation occurs because the molecules are constantly going back and forth between the two phases. This process is known as chromatography and is similar to what happens when a group of hikers start to climb a mountain. Some climb faster and some climb slower; the group spreads out based on the amount of time each individual takes.

Not all the marker dyes are mixtures, so sometimes you only observe one band of color. The dyes that are mixtures were designed to be certain colors not available from single dyes.

FOR THE RECORD

Molecules can be separated by chromatography based on their different physical properties.

TEST IT YOURSELF

Try this experiment using water instead of rubbing alcohol. Based on your observation, what does it mean when you say that a marker is "permanent"?

A.D.I.S.N. SAYS:

Chromatography isn't just a fancy-pants name! Chemical and biological research would be almost impossible without this technique. It's used extensively in laboratories to separate mixtures and purify materials. Pure compounds are important to study, because you need to know that the effects you observe are not caused by something else.

GENIUS

Section Two:
ADRIENNE ATTOMS

PRETTY BRILLIANT!

I was born a culinary chemist. My mother was a culinary chemist, and my abuelita, too, and my abuelita's mother and her abuelita's abuelita. You could say it's in my blood.

So . . . I know what you're thinking. *A culinary chemist? Is that actually a thing?* To that I say, absolutamente! It is definitely a thing. I love to experiment with science and cooking, and I create all my own recipes—everything from tasty shakes to beauty products. For example: my fingerprinting kit, which doubles as churro powder. It has cinnamon and sugar and flour. It can be used to dust a pen or a doorknob for prints from some crazy crook or evil villain. But I can also use it to top the most delectable fried dough you've ever tasted. Delicioso!

Then there are my signature brain-booster cookies. They help boost brain activity and sharpen decision making. They also happen to come in a variety of different flavors, like chocolate chunk chip or marshmallow mocha or mint mama (I named that one after Mamá, because she loves the taste of mint). Oh yum . . . I'm getting hungry just thinking about them.

Today I was in the NOV8 secret lab, mixing up some exploding glitter bath fizz, which is really just salt solution and CO_2 bubbles. It's like the old bath fizz I created, but with an extra secret ingredient—and did I mention mine are going to *explode*? And even better, they're going to have *glitter*? This bath fizz is a new beauty product I'm trying out. First I mixed the baking soda with Epsom salts. I took one teaspoon of silver glitter and mixed that in, too, then added another batch of baking soda.

That second batch of baking soda puts the *fizz* in bath fizz. Last but not least, I added my special secret ingredient to give it extra PIZZAZZ. (Okay, I can't keep a secret: It's food coloring!) I poured it into the circular mold I use for this recipe and let it set an hour. Then it was ready for its first test run.

I did some homework, then made some cookies, and the whole time the bath fizz was glittery pink and just sitting there on the lab desk, calling to me: *Adri! Try me out! Do a little test!* Por favor, mi amor! Por favor! So I decided to go searching for the perfect subjects. A little glitter never hurt anyone, right?

I crept out of the lab and found Bryden and McKeyla sitting in McKeyla's backyard. They were around her picnic table, drinking lemonade and talking about this device that Bryden's been working on. It changes your voice so you can sound like other people. Perfect for a mission, or some hilarious prank calls.

"How's your culinary chemistry going?" McKeyla asked when she saw me.

There was an outdoor fountain against the wall, just a few feet deep. I looked over at it and knew what I had to do. "Wanna see what I made?"

"Do I love my cell phone?" Bryden said.

"Of course," McKeyla added.

"Are you sure?" I said, giving them my cuter-than-cute smile.

"Show us! Now you have to!" They were practically yelling, so I thought, *Okay . . . If you insist,* mis amigas . . .

I grabbed the bath fizz and tossed it into the fountain. The pink powder hit the top of the water and then all I saw was an explosion of glitter. The foam went everywhere. It went all over McKeyla and Bryden, all over the table and A.D.I.S.N. and the patio chairs. Even the grass was covered.

A.D.I.S.N. made a surprised emoji face.

"Whoa!" Bryden said. "That works even better than the last version."

McKeyla wasn't even mad that I'd gotten bath fizz all over her black leather jacket and her new boots. She stood up and smiled. "You're a genius. This is the perfect distraction for when we're on a mission. If anyone is on to us, we can just throw some of this their way. Great work, Adri!"

I combed my hair with my hands, trying to get some of the foam out. "Why thank you, ladies," I said with a smile.

"Uh . . . Adri? You have a little something on your . . ." McKeyla pointed to my face.

I whipped out my compact mirror from my spy bag and held it up to the light. There was a giant streak of pink foam right over my top lip. It looked like a long, curling mustache!

So embarrassing. I ran to the bathroom to clean myself up— and to apply some crayon makeup and blush while I was at it.

For more culinary chemist recipes, take a look at some of my newest experiments!

ADRIENNE'S EXPERIMENTS

- Reflecting on Images

- Yeast Rises to the Challenge

- Sense of Smell

- Marvelous Morphing Marshmallows

- Cold and Colder

- Crystals Made to Order

REFLECTING
ON IMAGES

*Mirror, mirror on the wall,
who's the smartest of them all?*

MATERIALS

- ♡ 2 compact mirrors
- ♡ ruler
- ♡ 3 animal stickers
- ♡ shoe box
- ♡ pencil and paper

PROCEDURE

1. Open the compact mirrors so that the tops are completely vertical (at a 90° angle to the table). Measure the height.

2. Place one sticker in the middle of an inside short wall of the shoe box, half as high as the mirrors. Place a second sticker on one of the long walls, one mirror width from the short wall where you placed the first sticker. Place the third sticker exactly opposite the second sticker on the remaining long wall.

3. Using your pencil, punch a hole in one of the long walls half as high as the mirrors and one mirror width from the end without stickers.

4. Put one of the open mirror compacts in the box and try to place it so that you can see the sticker on the short wall through the hole. Note how you set the mirror and draw a diagram showing your line of sight to the mirror and then to the sticker.

5. Put both of the open mirror compacts in the box and try to place them in combination so that you can see one of the long wall stickers through the hole. Using your paper and pencil, note how you set the mirrors and draw a diagram showing your line of sight through the two mirrors to the sticker. Repeat with the other long wall sticker.

RESULTS

Light travels in straight lines, and a beam of light is called a ray. When a ray of light hits a reflecting surface at an angle, it bounces off at the same angle on the other side. You should be able to see this effect in your diagrams. Light from the sticker strikes the mirror and bounces off at the same angle on its way to your eye. The second mirror follows the same rule.

You most likely noticed that with one mirror, the sticker looked as if it had been reversed left to right (but not top to bottom). This is just an effect of how we perceive images reflected by mirrors—it hasn't been flipped, it just *looks* like it! When you used two mirrors, the orientation of the sticker appeared unchanged. This is because the second mirror reversed the effect of the first.

FOR THE RECORD

Mirrors reflect light at the same angle. Mirror images appear reversed from left to right but can be switched back with a second mirror.

TEST IT YOURSELF

If you write certain letters of the alphabet in block capitals and look at them in a mirror, you will see they are not reversed. This is because they are symmetrical. Can you identify all eleven of them?

A.D.I.S.N. SAYS:

Mirrors are extremely useful in many modern applications. Telescopes, lasers, and satellites all use them. It is the everyday uses, however, that most people know and enjoy. Especially fashionable people!

500ml
400
300
200

YEAST RISES
TO THE CHALLENGE

With a pinch of sugar—hold the spice!—and everything nice.

MATERIALS

- ♡ 3 balloons
- ♡ 3 clear plastic water bottles (empty)
- ♡ permanent marker
- ♡ measuring spoons
- ♡ 30 mL or 2 tbsp of sugar
- ♡ 30 mL or 2 tbsp of yeast
- ♡ 300 mL or 9 fl oz water
- ♡ 3 drinking glasses large enough to place the water bottles in

PROCEDURE

1 Blow up the balloons several times and practice stretching the open ends over the mouths of the empty water bottles.

2 Label the three bottles: (1) sugar, (2) yeast, and (3) sugar and yeast.

3 Add 15 mL (1 tbsp) of sugar to bottle #1. Add 15 mL (1 tbsp) of yeast to bottle #2. Add 15 mL (1 tbsp) each of sugar and yeast to bottle #3. Place the bottles in the glasses for stability.

4 Pour 100 mL (3 fl oz) of water into each of the bottles and seal them with balloons. Swirl each bottle gently.

5 After 30 minutes, record your observations in the table on the next page.

	CONTENTS	BALLOON SIZE	APPEARANCE OF MIXTURE
BOTTLE #1	SUGAR		
BOTTLE #2	YEAST		
BOTTLE #3	SUGAR + YEAST		

RESULTS

Yeasts are single-celled microorganisms found everywhere in the world. They get their energy to grow mostly from breaking down sugars, which releases water (H_2O) and carbon dioxide (CO_2). Carbon dioxide is a gas, so it expands inside the bottle. Because the bottle in this experiment is sealed, the rise in pressure causes the balloon to inflate. Leaving out one ingredient in each of the other bottles lets you be sure that it is the combination of the yeast and sugar that is necessary.

Comparisons like these are called "control experiments" and are important if you want to make sound conclusions.

FOR THE RECORD

Yeast is a single-celled microorganism that consumes sugar and generates carbon dioxide.

TEST IT YOURSELF

Sugars are also called carbohydrates. There are many different kinds of carbohydrates in the food we eat. Some are simple, like regular sugar (sucrose) or honey (glucose and fructose). Others are more complex, like corn or potatoes, which are made up of many simple sugars joined together. What do you think would happen if you tried to feed yeast with some of these?

A.D.I.S.N. SAYS:

Yeast is used to bake many different types of bread that we eat. The carbon dioxide produced by combining yeast and sugar makes tiny bubbles in the dough. When we bake the dough, the bubbles give the bread its soft and spongy texture that everyone goes on and on about. Not that I can try it.

Even the Egyptians were raving about it! Ancient drawings and artifacts show they knew about yeast and were baking bread 4,000 years ago!

SENSE OF SMELL

The nose knows.

MATERIALS

♡ large sheet of paper

♡ marker

♡ modeling clay

♡ 5–6 buttons of various sizes and shapes

♡ toothpick

♡ several flavor extracts, such as lemon, mint, almond, or vanilla

PROCEDURE

1. Draw the outline of a nose in profile on the sheet of paper.

2. Make several circular cookie shapes about 5 cm (2 in) across and about 1 cm (½ in) thick from the modeling clay. Take the buttons and press one into each modeling clay disk, then remove the buttons carefully. The toothpick can be used to ease each button out so its impression is not distorted.

With the toothpick, inscribe the underside of each modeling clay impression with the initial of a fragrance. Then put a few drops of the matching flavor extract on the corresponding button.

4 Test your sense of smell: Place the modeling clay disks on the drawing of the nose. Line up the buttons in front of you. Sniff each button and then match it with its impression. Flip over the modeling clay impressions and see if the inscriptions match the fragrances of the disks.

OBSERVATIONS AND RESULTS

A smell is simply small molecules that float up in the air from different sources and end up in your nose. They are usually mixtures with many components, and the way the components smell depends on their shape.

- The smell of a lemon is due in part to limonene.
- Mint depends on menthol for its distinctive aroma.
- The odor of almonds comes from benzaldehyde.
- The main component of vanilla is a molecule called vanillin.

You can see the different shapes of these molecules in the pictures below:

LIMONENE

MENTHOL

BENZALDEHYDE

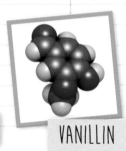

VANILLIN

Your ability to tell different smells apart depends on olfactory cells in your nose. Each olfactory cell has a receptor that can recognize only one type of molecule. It does this by shape, like a lock that only one type of key can open. When a molecule of the right shape lands in a receptor, the cell sends a signal to the brain.

There are about 400 different types of receptors in your nose. Each odor interacts with a different combination of them—that is why you can recognize so many different smells.

FOR THE RECORD

Smells are just small molecules floating in the air. The nose has special cells that recognize them based on their shape. Some noses, however, are particularly attuned to sniffing out churros!

TEST IT YOURSELF

Water is made of very small molecules, and there are plenty of them floating in the air. Does water have a smell? If you think it does, how would you know it's not just something dissolved in the water? If you think it doesn't, why wouldn't it?

A.D.I.S.N. SAYS:

To understand our world we use five senses: sight, hearing, touch, taste, and smell. Special scientists called neuroscientists have learned that smell and memory are related. Smell, not sight or hearing, brings back our memory quickly: You smell salt water and think of a trip to the beach.

Scientists are also starting to use smell training to help improve memories. The next time that delicious aroma wafts through Adrienne's kitchen, you'll not only have an amazing meal, you'll have an amazing memory! (But I'll have to hear you go *on and on* about it, because I can't taste anything!)

MARVELOUS MORPHING
MARSHMALLOWS

Delicioso and brilliant.

THIS
EXPERIMENT
REQUIRES ADULT
SUPERVISION.

MATERIALS

- ♡ 5 marshmallows
- ♡ 5 small paper plates
- ♡ microwave oven
- ♡ ruler

PROCEDURE

1. Place one marshmallow on each of 5 plates.

2. Ask an adult to heat each marshmallow for a different length of time: 0, 10, 20, 30, and 40 seconds.

3. Write down your observations. How did the marshmallows change? You can make a table and, using your ruler, record the size, shape, and color in each case.

OBSERVATIONS

TIME	0 SECONDS	10 SECONDS	20 SECONDS	30 SECONDS	40 SECONDS
SIZE					
SHAPE					
COLOR					

RESULTS

The main solid ingredient in a marshmallow is sugar, but the marshmallow itself is mostly air. It's like a tasty sponge with millions of tiny bubbles that make it soft and springy. The microwave oven heats the little bit of water in the sugary mixture, which in turn heats up the air bubbles and causes them to expand rapidly. The gooey, delicious-looking mixture puffs up and out as the pockets of air get bigger, but collapses as the bubbles break and the air escapes. After that, the sugar starts to burn.

FOR THE RECORD

Gases expand when heated and contract when cooled.

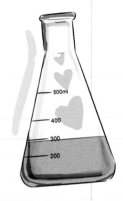

TEST IT YOURSELF

In this experiment, why was there one marshmallow that you didn't heat?

A.D.I.S.N. SAYS:

You should be thinking, *Gases expand when heated,* every time you see a volcano. And you should think of me, telling you that. Actually, you should just think of me always!

COLD
AND COLDER

I scream for ice cream!

MATERIALS

- ♡ 250 mL or 8 fl oz of half-and-half (milk and cream)
- ♡ 30 mL or 2 tbsp of sugar
- ♡ dash of vanilla extract
- ♡ 1 large and 1 small sealable plastic bag
- ♡ 30 ice cubes
- ♡ outdoor thermometer
- ♡ 125 mL or 8 tbsp of salt
- ♡ towel

PROCEDURE

1 Combine 250 mL (8 fl oz) of half-and-half (milk and cream) with 30 mL (2 tbsp) of sugar and a dash of vanilla extract in the small sealable plastic bag. Minimize trapped air when sealing.

2 Place about 30 ice cubes in the large sealable plastic bag. Measure the temperature and record it in the table. Add 125 mL (4 fl oz) of salt and mix together for one minute. Measure the temperature again.

ADULTS ONLY FOR THIS STEP!

MAKE SURE TO NOT TOUCH THE ICE-SALT DIRECTLY—IT'S SO COLD, IT'S POSSIBLE TO BURN YOURSELF!

3 Place the small bag in the large bag and close it. Minimize trapped air when sealing. Wrap the bag in a towel and gently knead for about 5 minutes. Open the large bag and measure the temperature one more time. Check to see if the mixture in the small bag has thickened and turned into ice cream. If not, close the bag and continue kneading. If yes, rinse off the small bag and serve. Enjoy!

TIME POINT	TEMPERATURE °C / °F
ICE ONLY	
ICE AND SALT, 1 MINUTE	
ICE AND SALT, 5 MINUTES	

RESULTS

When you dissolve salt in water, the resulting mixture has a lower freezing point than the pure water. This is because the two kinds of molecules arrange themselves differently when they are together. Energy is pulled from the surroundings to accomplish this, so the cold mixture gets colder.

FOR THE RECORD

Adding salt to ice lowers the temperature of the mixture below the freezing point of water. You can use any solid that dissolves in water to do this—it doesn't have to be a specific chemical compound!

TEST IT YOURSELF

Why do we need temperatures lower than the freezing point of water to make ice cream?

A.D.I.S.N. SAYS:

Every liquid has its own freezing point. Pure water freezes at 0°C/32°F. Sometimes it's useful to alter that freezing point. Salt lowers the freezing point of water and causes ice and snow to melt. Roads are salted in the winter so ice won't form, cars don't skid and cause accidents, and people don't slip.

It's better than shoveling. I know that, and technically I'm a notebook!

CRYSTALS
MADE TO ORDER

Show off your best side(s). . . .

THIS EXPERIMENT REQUIRES ADULT SUPERVISION.

MATERIALS

- ♡ 60 grams (g) or 4 tbsp of borax
- ♡ 250 mL or 8 fl oz of hot water
- ♡ clear plastic cups
- ♡ food coloring (optional)
- ♡ string, wire, or pipe cleaners
- ♡ pencils
- ♡ paper towels
- ♡ ruler

PROCEDURE

1 Dissolve 60 g (4 tbsp) of borax in 250 mL (8 fl oz) of hot water. Pour into a clear plastic cup, and if desired, add a few drops of food coloring.

2 Tie a piece of string to the middle of a pencil and place it on top of the cup so that the string dangles in the solution. You may choose to use wires or pipe cleaners bent into different shapes instead. Crystals may start forming within an hour, but allow the mixture to stand at room temperature for 24 hours.

3 After you remove the crystal-encrusted string, dip it briefly in a glass of plain water and dry it gently with a paper towel.

4 Look closely at the individual crystals and note their shape and sizes. Try to draw a three-dimensional picture of one on the facing page. Then draw a line as wide as your sketch underneath, and mark the ends with short vertical lines. Use a ruler to measure the actual crystal and record the measurements below the line. Now you have a "scale drawing" of your crystal!

5 If desired, make additional batches using different colors. Larger shapes work best and you will need to use several drops of food coloring. Throw out the crystals when you're done.

OBSERVATIONS

Draw to scale a crystal you just produced!

RESULTS

You may have noticed that it is easier to dissolve things in hot water than cold.

When solid borax is dissolved in hot water, the molecules of borax move faster and farther apart from one another. As the hot water cools, the dissolved molecules slow down and move closer to each other. The molecules eventually start sticking together, forming solid crystals. Once the first crystals have formed, it becomes easier for additional molecules to join them, which makes the crystals larger. Having a string or wire in the solution provides a rough surface that helps the first crystals form.

Borax is a naturally occurring mineral, which means it is not man-made. It is mined from the earth and looks like a white spiky rock. Borax is a common name for the chemical sodium tetraborate decahydrate, which has a chemical formula of $Na_2B_4O_7 \cdot 10H_2O$. Some substances have common names that are easier to remember and say, but the chemical name provides information about what atoms make up the compound. Borax is used in the cleaning and chemical industries and also for arts and crafts projects!

FOR THE RECORD

Dissolving certain compounds in hot water-based liquids and allowing the liquid to cool or evaporate can grow crystals.

TEST IT YOURSELF

How easily crystals form depends on the shape of the individual molecules and how readily they fit together. What might you expect to happen if you used another substance such as salt or sugar in the hot water solution instead of borax?

A.D.I.S.N. SAYS:

What's fascinating about crystals is that a single microscopic crystal of borax has the same shape as the large borax crystals you made. The diameter of a molecule of borax is itty-bitty— it measures about 0.000000001 meter across (a nanometer), but the minuscule crystals that are formed first set the pattern for the shape of the large crystals that we can see.

The idea of building or assembling matter at the nanometer level is what nanotechnology is all about. I already knew that, of course—but you're welcome for the information. I just made you smarter!

Section Three:
BRYDEN BANDWETH

STAND
Back...
i'm trending.

#

Okay, so maybe most people would look at a computer screen full of code and their eyes would start watering and their head would start spinning and they'd just think it was line after line of numbers, letters, and symbols that were such total nonsense. I get it. But for a serious coder like me it's like looking at a big puzzle with all these unique pieces in it. There's a way to make everything fit together and work, and it's up to you to figure out how.

This afternoon I finished the code for the new device I'm working on. If I let Camryn name it, it would be called something like the Voice-Altering Necklace Device That Changes Your Voice to Make It Sound Like Someone Else's (she's great at inventing things, but not so great at naming inventions). For right now I'm just calling it a Voice-Altering Necklace. Basically I want to be able to take recordings of anyone's voice and create a code that would alter my voice to sound like theirs, with all the different tones and inflections that make it unique. I started with Adrienne's voice just to see if it would work. But eventually I want to write code for a few hackers that have attacked NOV8. Being able to impersonate their voices could help us on one of our missions, and maybe even get some top secret information.

I pulled up the recordings of Adrienne's voice. I had stopped by Café Attoms yesterday and recorded her talking to customers for a whole hour. Then I spent all night writing code to mimic her voice. I put the final finishing touches on the code, and it seemed like everything was working the way it should. I listened again to a few clips of the recordings just to make sure I could hear Adrienne's real voice clearly as a comparison.

"Welcome to Café Attoms! Would you like to try our new signature drink? I call it . . . the churrochino!" Adrienne's voice came out of my computer speakers.

She's pretty much the perkiest person I know. I talk super fast and would say I'm in a good mood most of the time, but I couldn't imagine being that excited and happy every minute of every day. I wanted to see if my device could at least make me *sound* like Adrienne. Bubbly and full of life.

I picked up the necklace off my desk. I'd made it a choker so that it would sit high on my neck but didn't feel too tight, close enough to my vocal cords to alter the pitch and tone of everything I said without being too restrictive. I adjusted it and then leaned in. . . .

"Welcome to Café Attoms," I said. "My name is Adrienne Attoms and I'm a culinary chemist, and yes! That is totally a thing!"

I pulled the necklace off, totally freaked out. I sounded exactly like Adrienne! I'd been able to capture her voice perfectly!

"That is seriously freaky," I said to myself.

Sure, it sounded right to me, but would I be able to fool someone else into thinking I was Adrienne? Like one of our friends? That would be much harder.

I put the necklace back on and dialed McKeyla, making sure to block my number so she wouldn't know it was me. It rang twice before McKeyla answered.

"Hello?"

"McKeyla, it's Adri!" I said, the necklace making me sound exactly like Adrienne. "I was thinking . . ." Then I blanked on what to say.

"You were thinking . . ."

Was McKeyla onto me? I should've planned this out better! "I was thinking—about food."

"You're always thinking about food."

"Yeah, that's me. Totally an Adri thing to think about food!" I forced a laugh that sounded so much like Adrienne's, I impressed myself. "Just trying out some new brain-booster cookie recipes. I want you to try them when you come by the café next. What do you think? How does that *sound*?"

"Great idea. I love your recipes."

"So that *sounds* okay? *I* sound okay?"

"Yeah . . . but you're being a little weird. What's up?"

I unhooked the necklace and cleared my throat.

"It's actually me—Bry. I was testing out my newest invention—that voice-altering necklace I told you about. I think we can use it to impersonate the hackers' voices."

"Whoa . . . I totally thought you were Adri. You sounded just like her."

"It's good, huh? I wrote code based on recordings I had of her voice." I couldn't help but smile.

"It's really good. Just let me know when the device is fully ready. The Quail will be so impressed."

"You got it." Then we said our good-byes and hung up.

I pulled up another screen, typing in the beginning of the code I'd used for Adrienne's voice. If we had audio recordings of any future suspects, I could create a code based on the words they used in conversation.

To learn more about code, as well as some of my other favorite things, including sound and circuits, check out the steps below.

BRYDEN'S EXPERIMENTS

DISCLAIMER This experiment should be conducted under adult supervision. Never use a battery with a voltage higher than 1.5. Follow wiring instructions carefully; incorrect wiring can result in battery leakage and/or rupture. DO NOT take a battery apart, dispose in fire, or recharge. This may cause batteries to explode, leak, and cause injury.

LET'S CONNECT

. . . and go with the flow (of electrons)!

THIS EXPERIMENT REQUIRES ADULT ASSISTANCE.

MATERIALS

★ 40 cm or 16 in of flexible insulated copper wire

★ wire cutter and stripper

★ 3 small metal paper clips

★ masking tape

★ 2–3 volt flashlight bulb

★ 1 cm x 5 cm or ½ in x 2 in wide rubber band

★ 1.5 volt battery (AA or AAA, new and to be used according to manufacturer's instructions)

★ several metallic and nonmetallic objects

PROCEDURE

1 Cut the copper wire in half and strip off about 2 cm (¾ in) of insulation from all four ends.

2 Attach a paper clip to three of the four bare wire ends by wrapping the exposed flexible wire through and around one loop of a paper clip several times.

3 Lay the remaining bare wire end on a piece of masking tape 1 cm x 3 cm (½ in x 1 in) lengthwise and wrap the tape around the cylindrical base of the flashlight bulb so that the bare wire is touching the metal. The bottom tip of the lightbulb should remain exposed. Now you have one wire with two paper clip ends, and one wire with a paper clip at one end and a lightbulb at the other.

4 Place the wide rubber band around the battery lengthwise so it covers the terminals. It should be a snug fit. Slip one paper clip from one wire under the rubber band at one end of the battery so that the clip is held tightly against the terminals. Place a paper clip from the second wire under the rubber band on the opposite battery terminal so it's also held tightly. The conductivity tester is now ready.

5 Check the conductivity tester by touching the free paper clip end to the bottom tip of the lightbulb. It should light up.

6 Test several objects to see if they conduct electricity by touching them with the paper clip and the bottom tip of the lightbulb at the same time. If the light comes on, the object is a conductor of electricity. If it does not, the object is an insulator. Record your observations in the table on the next page.

OBSERVATIONS

CONDUCTORS	INSULATORS

RESULTS

Electrons are small, negatively charged particles that revolve around the nucleus of an atom at incredibly high speeds. Some types of atoms, however, do not hold on to their electrons very tightly. These electrons can jump from one atom to another with ease.

One end of a battery has a supply of extra electrons (negative terminal). The other end is deficient in electrons (positive terminal). The electrons, however, can't get from one end to the other unless the terminals are joined with a material that allows the electrons to jump from atom to atom and "flow" through it. Such a material is called a conductor. Many metals, such as iron, copper, and aluminum are extremely good conductors. This flow of electrons is what we call electricity. A material in which electrons do not jump readily from one atom to another is called an insulator. Glass, rubber, and wood are examples of good insulators.

When you tested a conductor, electrons were able to flow from one end of the battery through both the light and the test material and then back into the battery. The light turned on! When you tested an insulator, the flow of electrons was interrupted, and the light remained off.

FOR THE RECORD

Materials that allow electrons to flow are called conductors.
The flow of electrons through conductors is called electricity.
Materials that do not allow electrons to flow are called insulators.

TEST IT YOURSELF

Some conductors are better than others. How might that affect the light given off by your conductivity tester?

A.D.I.S.N. SAYS:

The trick to using electricity is to control where it goes—and that's where conductors and insulators come in. One provides a road for electrons and the other provides a curb that keeps them on track. The electric grid that supplies our homes, schools, and businesses depends on thousands and thousands of kilometers (miles) of insulated wiring—and it keeps me nice and charged so I can correct you whenever you're wrong!

CIRCUITS
AT WORK

Get with the program!

MATERIALS

- ★ hole punch
- ★ 20 cm x 30 cm or 8 in x 12 in thin cardboard
- ★ Eight 4 cm x 30 cm or 1½ in x 12 in strips of aluminum foil
- ★ conductivity tester (from Bryden's "Let's Connect" Experiment)
- ★ masking tape
- ★ scissors
- ★ marker pen
- ★ set of questions and answers

PROCEDURE

1 Punch eight holes down each of the long sides of the cardboard about 2 cm (¾ in) in from the edges and 3 cm (1 in) apart. The holes should line up in pairs across the page.

2 Fold eight 4 cm x 30 cm (1½ in x 12 in) strips of aluminum foil in half twice the long way so you end up with eight strips that are about 1 cm x 30 cm (½ in x 12 in) strips.

3 Lay a strip so that it covers one hole on the left side and one on the right side at the same time. The holes should not be directly across from each other, so it will lay across the board on a diagonal. Using a long piece of masking tape, cover and stick the entire aluminum strip to the cardboard. Make sure, however, that you can see the aluminum foil through the holes on the other side.

4 Repeat with the other seven aluminum strips till all the holes are connected in pairs. Keep track of which holes are joined to each other. Trim excess aluminum foil and masking tape from around the edge of the cardboard.

5 Flip the cardboard over and write a question next to each of the holes on the left. Write answers next to the holes on the right. Make sure that a strip of aluminum foil connects each question-and-answer pair. You have now "programmed" your computer.

Time to "turn on" your computer and try it out: Use the conductivity tester to match answers with questions. Touch one end of the tester to a hole next to a question and find the corresponding answer by touching holes next to the answers with the other end. If you match the correct answer, the conductivity tester light will turn on.

 If desired, make additional sets of questions and answers on separate sheets of paper and lay them on top of your computer, lining up the holes.

OBSERVATIONS AND RESULTS

Whenever you matched a question and answer, you completed a circuit. Electricity was able to flow from the battery along a strip of aluminum foil in your computer, through the light, and back to the battery.

What makes your device a computer is that you assigned a meaning to a circuit that was complete or "on" (correct answer) and a meaning to a circuit that was not complete or "off" (incorrect answer). Computer engineers refer to this as a *binary code* and use either a 0 (off) or a 1 (on) to indicate the two possibilities. Modern computers are able to make millions of these types of decisions in fractions of seconds, enabling all the programs and applications that our world now runs on. Your computer has only eight circuits, but you can already see how useful it is as a simple teaching device.

FOR THE RECORD

Computers rely on circuits that are either on (1) or off (0). Information can be programmed into them using this binary code.

TEST IT YOURSELF

Why did you need to use masking tape in building this computer? What other material could you have used in place of the aluminum foil?

A.D.I.S.N. SAYS:

Computers are everywhere. They are in our homes, schools, and workplaces. They provide tremendous convenience and put information at our fingertips (and keep Bryden glued to her screen all hours of the day!). Their usefulness, however, depends on how well we understand how they work— knowing what a circuit is is just the beginning!

LIGHT:
A COLORFUL CHARACTER

Mix it up for a brand-new hue!

MATERIALS

* ★ red, blue, and green tissue paper
* ★ 3 identical LED flashlights
* ★ rubber bands
* ★ colored pencils
* ★ a dark room
* ★ a white sheet of paper (like printer paper)

1 Double the thickness of each piece of tissue paper and cover the lens of each flashlight with a different color. Use the rubber bands to hold the tissue paper in place. You will have a flashlight covered in red, a flashlight covered in blue, and a flashlight covered in green tissue paper when you are done.

2 Color in the red, blue, and green sections that don't overlap in the diagram below.

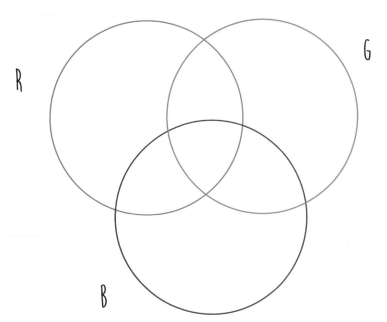

3 You will need to work in a dark room, but before you turn off all the lights, place a sheet of white paper on the table.

Hold the red flashlight in one hand and the green one in the other. Shine the colored circles of light side by side on the sheet of paper and slowly bring them together. Color in the appropriate overlapping space in the diagram on the previous page.

 Repeat the experiment with the green and blue flashlights. Color in the appropriate overlapping space in the diagram.

 Repeat the experiment with the blue and red flashlights. Color in the appropriate overlapping space in the diagram.

 With the help of a friend, bring the colored beams of all three flashlights together on the paper. Note the result in the diagram on the previous page.

OBSERVATIONS AND RESULTS

Visible light is a form of energy that our eyes can detect. Our eyes have color-sensing cells in the retina called cones that respond to different colors of light. When different colors of light are mixed together, our eyes sense the new combination and the brain interprets it as a different color.

If you start with a set of three primary colors, you can mix them in different amounts and get a full range of colors that correspond quite well to those found in nature. Primary colors produce white light when all three are combined with the right intensity. A common set of primary colors are red, blue, and green. When combined systematically, they produce a set of secondary colors: cyan, magenta, and yellow. These are the colors you observed and colored in the overlap diagram on page 93. When all three colors overlapped correctly, you saw white—so the center of the overlap diagram did not need to be colored.

$$R + G = YELLOW$$

$$G + B = CYAN$$

$$B + R = MAGENTA$$

$$R + B + G = WHITE$$

You probably noticed that you could vary the brightness of the lights by raising and lowering the flashlights shining on the paper. This in turn changed the color of the overlapping circle of light.

FOR THE RECORD

The light we see is usually a mixture of colors. You can make a full range of colors using only the three primary colors: red, blue, and green. When all three are present in the right proportion, you get white light.

A.D.I.S.N. SAYS:

Different colors of light can be combined to make new colors. Primary colors are used to produce all the full-color images on our television, computer, camera, and—ahem—tablet screens. (Why do you think I'm so awesomely rendered?)

TEST IT YOURSELF

Would changing the thickness of the tissue paper give different colors?

Would different combinations of paper on the flashlight make different colors?

Would you get similar results using paints instead of light in this experiment?

SETTING
THE (PERIODIC) TABLE

What's the matter?

oxygen	magnesium
8	12
O	**Mg**
15.999	24.305

MATERIALS

★ diagram of element cubes

★ periodic table

PROCEDURE

1 Samples of five elements are shown in the diagram below and labeled with their atomic number. Write the numbers in the observation table.

13   26   29   30   82

2 With the atomic number, you can figure out the chemical symbol for each element by finding it in the periodic table. Record them in the observations table.

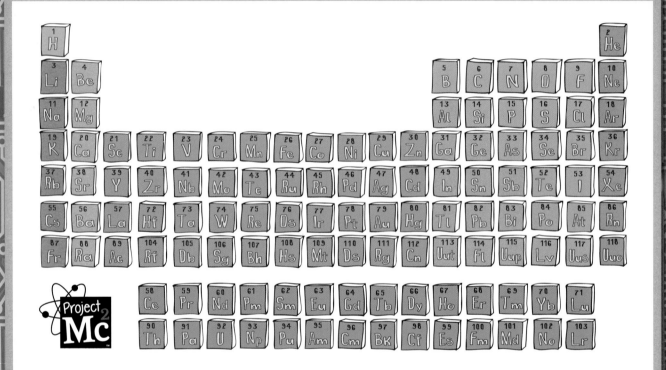

3 The chemical symbol in the above chart is just an abbreviation for the actual name of the element. Your mission is to find the full names by looking them up in the library or online! Scientists publish their work so other scientists can learn from their experiments and findings, and build on them. Researching is a great way to learn, get inspired, and think up new ideas!

copper
29
Cu
63.546

tellurium
52
Te
127.60

ATOMIC NUMBER	CHEMICAL SYMBOL	CHEMICAL NAME

RESULTS

Each chemical element is identified by the number of protons in the center of its atom, which is called the nucleus. Hydrogen (H) has an atomic number of 1, which means it has 1 proton in its nucleus. Bromine (Br) has 35 protons. The elements are then organized in a table according to this number, going from left to right in successive rows. Notice, for example, that elements 29 and 30 in your observation table are right next to each other. It's called the periodic table because certain properties of the elements repeat "periodically" as you move down rows.

FOR THE RECORD

Elements are identified by the number of protons in their atoms, which is called the atomic number. Elements are organized by their atomic number in the periodic table.

TEST IT YOURSELF

Why isn't the chemical symbol simply the first two letters of an element's name?

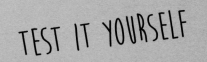

A.D.I.S.N. SAYS:

The periodic table is very useful because elements above and below have similar properties. Did you notice the elements chosen for this experiment are all common metals? Some precious metals, like gold, silver, and even platinum, are found in everyday electronics—like me!

Which means that I am precious! (You can also do what Bryden does with the periodic table and use chemical symbols to make cool catchphrases! OMG!)

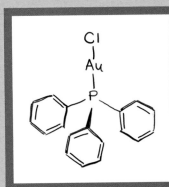

PANPIPE
PANDEMONIUM

EDM isn't the only music out there!

THIS EXPERIMENT REQUIRES ADULT ASSISTANCE.

MATERIALS

- ★ 60 cm (2 ft) of 1¼ cm (½ in) CTS CPVC plastic pipe or PVC Schedule 40 plastic pipe
- ★ hacksaw (adult use only!)
- ★ ruler and pencil
- ★ sandpaper
- ★ steel wool
- ★ masking tape
- ★ colored markers and/or colored yarn (optional)

PROCEDURE

1 To make a set of panpipes, ask an adult to cut five pieces of plastic pipe to the following lengths: 154 mm (6$\frac{1}{16}$ in), 137 mm (5$\frac{3}{8}$ in), 121 mm (4$\frac{3}{4}$ in), 98 mm (3$\frac{7}{8}$ in), and 87 mm (3$\frac{7}{16}$ in). Be careful to make straight 90° cuts. Smooth the ends with sandpaper, and if desired, remove writing with steel wool. (*Almond-colored CTS CPVC pipe is narrower and easier to play, but regular PVC pipe works well, too.*)

ADULTS ONLY FOR THIS STEP!

2 Seal one end of each tube with a short strip of masking tape pulled as tautly as possible over the opening. Add a second layer. Wrap a strip of masking tape around the end of the tube to secure and hide the edges of the masking tape covering the hole.

3 Test each pipe to make sure you get a good tone. Touch the edge of the open end of each tube lightly to your lower lip and blow across the top at an angle. If necessary, adjust the masking tape until you get a good sound.

4 If desired, decorate the tubes using colored markers. The tubes correspond to the following notes (longest to shortest): C, D, E, G, and A.

Lay the tubes on a table and line up the open ends. Tape them together about 2 cm (1 in) below the tube ends with a strip of masking tape, going around at least twice. Repeat a few centimeters (an inch or so) lower so that the pipes are held securely.

 Your panpipes are ready to play! You should be able to get a nice tone from each pipe, although the shorter ones are harder. You can decorate the panpipes at this point, too, by drawing designs on the masking tape or wrapping a band of colored yarn around the middle like they do in South America.

 Once you are able to play the notes, you can try to play this familiar tune: EDCD EEE DDD EGG EDCD EEEE DDED C.

 If you add more notes, you can play more tunes. Here are three more pipe sizes that will help you do this by playing notes F, B, and high C: 113 mm ($4\frac{7}{16}$ in), 75 mm ($2\frac{15}{16}$ in), and 71 mm ($2\frac{13}{16}$ in).

Blow across the top of each of your pipes. How does the length of the pipe affect how low or high it sounds?

Sound is the back-and-forth movement of air particles caused by a vibrating object. You hear sounds because your ear can detect these vibrations moving through the air. When you blow across the top of one of the pipes, you are causing the air molecules to vibrate inside the tube. You can feel this if you put your finger on the closed end while you blow.

The number of vibrations you get every second is called the frequency, and the frequency depends on the length of the pipe. Every pipe has its own natural frequency—the longer ones have fewer vibrations per second and the shorter ones have more. In music, frequency is called pitch and certain special frequencies are called notes. These have specific names: C, D, E, G, and A, among others.

FOR THE RECORD

Sound is the vibration of air particles detected by your ear. A long column of air produces a low sound (low frequency), and a short column of air produces a high sound (high frequency).

TEST IT YOURSELF

Which instrument makes a higher-pitched sound—a piccolo or a flute? A violin or a cello? Can you explain why?

NEXT LEVEL

A.D.I.S.N. SAYS:

Sound is important for communication, and it also allows humans to create music. Musical notes are produced by vibrating air particles in many different ways—from hitting a drum or plucking a string to blowing through a trumpet. We also use electronics to simulate these sounds and some awesome dance beats. What else do you think Bryden has blasting through her headphones?

PICTURE THIS:
STARS IN MOTION

If you're seeing stars . . . everything is fine!

MATERIALS

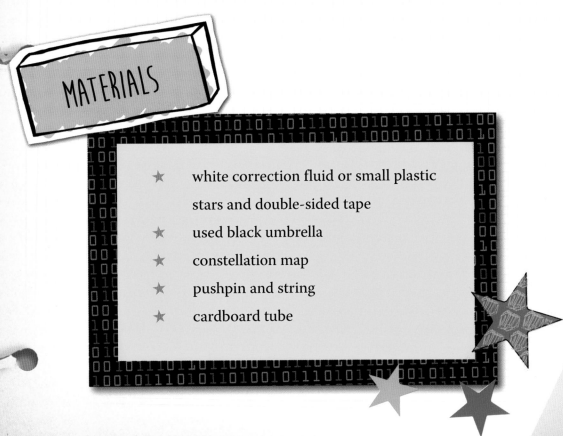

- ★ white correction fluid or small plastic stars and double-sided tape
- ★ used black umbrella
- ★ constellation map
- ★ pushpin and string
- ★ cardboard tube

PROCEDURE

1 Using the white correction fluid, paint the star constellations inside the open black umbrella according to the star chart below. One quick dab per star is all that is needed. The umbrella handle attaches to the "sky" through the North Star. This is the star at the tip of Ursa Minor, the constellation also known as the Little Dipper. Don't draw any of the lines. (If you use small plastic stars and double-sided tape instead of correction fluid, you will be able to return the umbrella to its original condition at the end of the experiment.)

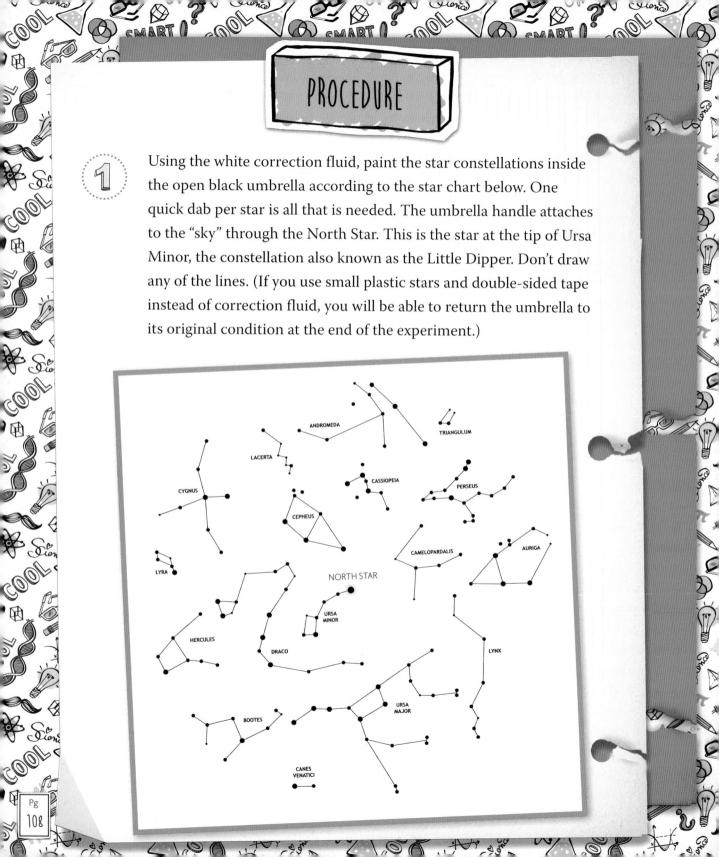

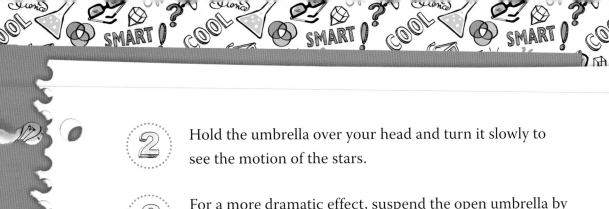

2 Hold the umbrella over your head and turn it slowly to see the motion of the stars.

3 For a more dramatic effect, suspend the open umbrella by its tip in a doorway using a loop of string and a pushpin. Give the umbrella a gentle twirl and lie down underneath it looking up. The twist in the string will slowly unwind and rotate the "sky." Use the cardboard tube like a telescope and keep the "North Star" in your field of view.

OBSERVATIONS AND RESULTS

You may have noticed that the stars appear to move throughout the night. If you observe more closely, you will see that the stars appear to rotate around a single star. That star is called Polaris, also known as the North Star.

The stars, however, don't really move. We are the ones who are actually moving, due to the rotation of the earth. As our planet turns, different stars come into view. The effect is similar to what happens when you sit on a merry-go-round and watch the surroundings go by.

The earth spins around its axis, the ends of which we call the North and South Poles. The North Star does not appear to move because it happens to be directly over the North Pole. In our umbrella model, you have to imagine the umbrella handle sticking up out of the North Pole and connecting to the sky at the North Star. Complex computer models now track the skies. By spinning the handle to simulate the rotation of the earth, we can look through our cardboard "telescope" to see the stars in the umbrella move in the same way the real ones appear to move in the sky.

FOR THE RECORD

The stars appear to rotate around the North Star due to the rotation of the earth. The North Star lies directly over the North Pole.

TEST IT YOURSELF

Knowing that the North Star lies directly over the North Pole means that it is a good way to tell which way north is. Why can't you always rely on this method to find your way?

A.D.I.S.N. SAYS:

Understanding how our planet moves in space is the first step in understanding our relationship to the stars and galaxies. It also lets us do practical things such as launch satellites that help us communicate around the world—like interplanetary texting!

Section Four:
CAMRYN COYLE

NAILED IT!

<3

The only thing better than a hoverboard is a High-Tech, Super-Powered Hoverboard with Upgraded Thermal Booster. I've been working on my upgrade for months now, tweaking the latest version I made and trying to get it just right. I stayed up late to finish it, but then the unthinkable happened: I broke the thermal booster on the back of the board.

So I woke up early this morning to fix it. Early enough that the sky was still dark. I had just two hours before I had to get dressed and go to school, so I sat down at my workbench and grabbed my screwdriver and tried my best to get the booster working again. The booster pack sits on the back of the hoverboard. It's filled with wires, and a small battery that gives it its power. When I switched the old booster on, I could go about three miles per hour. But my new and improved booster help me go at least double that.

The problem wasn't the easiest to fix. I checked and double-checked all the wiring to make sure nothing had gone wrong there (it hadn't). All the wires were connected to all the right entry points. Then I checked the battery to make sure that wasn't the problem either (it wasn't). It was a brand-new one. I'd been really excited to take this hoverboard on its very first test ride, and I'd decided today was the day. But after an hour I wasn't feeling too hopeful.

Then . . . it happened. I had a major breakthrough. I was staring off into space (something I do when I'm trying to puzzle out an engineering problem) and I suddenly realized I was staring at this industrial-size magnet on the corner of my workbench. I remembered that last night, right before the booster mysteriously stopped working, I'd set the hoverboard down next to it. The booster was only an inch or two away. I wondered if maybe the magnetic charge had thrown the circuitry in the booster off. I went through, replacing the wires one by one, and then I turned it back on. It totally worked! Within minutes, the booster was fastened on my hoverboard again and I was ready to take my latest invention for a spin.

I got dressed, threw on my helmet, elbow pads, and knee pads, and stood at the edge of my driveway, my foot on my board. Then I pushed off, careening out into the street. I built some momentum and got myself up to a decent speed before reaching down and turning on the booster. Soon I was moving twice as fast as before. My neighborhood flew past, house after house. I didn't have to do anything except steer myself. I leaned forward to turn toward school.

As I got closer, all the kids spun around to see my approach. I must've been moving even faster than I thought I was, because people started cheering. One girl even raised her hand and made that *rock on!* sign. I flew up the ramp toward the main entrance, and a boy with purple hair opened the door for me so I could zoom right through. At the end of the hall, I pushed back on my board, popping it up into my hand.

"Nailed it!" I said. I glanced around at the crowd that had already formed on all sides of me. A group of girls clapped. Everyone seemed beyond impressed.

Too bad I hadn't noticed Assistant Principal Wilson standing behind me.

"You also ruined your Saturday, speed queen. See you in detention," he said.

As he walked away, I stared down at the hoverboard in my hand. The boosters were still too hot to touch, and I could feel the heat from just a few inches away. I'd never invented something with so much power before. If everyone at school started using my High-Tech Super-Powered Hoverboard with Upgraded Thermal Booster (I'm good at inventing, not so great at naming the inventions) kids would get there in half the time.

Okay, maybe I'd ruined a perfectly good weekend.

But it was totally, truly worth it—I just had the best test ride of my life! And anyway, my hoverboard would be useful for doing surveillance for NOV8, *off* campus of course.

Check out some of my favorite inventions in the experiment section on the next page. . . .

CAMRYN'S EXPERIMENTS

- Skateboard on the Slopes

- You've Got the Motion

- The Layered Look

- Blast Off!

- Sand's Hot, Water's Not

- Getting in Shape: Geodesic Domes

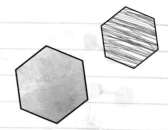

SKATEBOARD
ON THE SLOPES

If you have the need for speed . . . and energy.

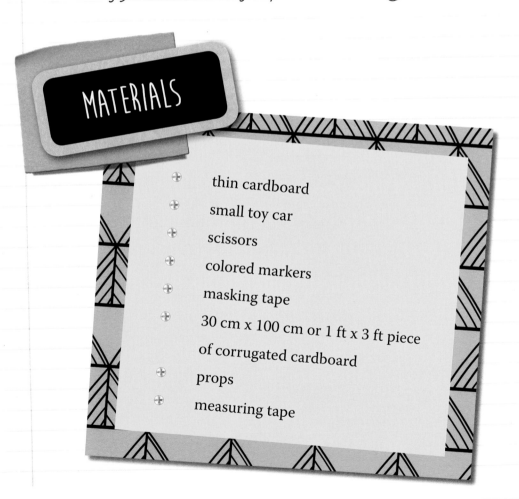

MATERIALS

- thin cardboard
- small toy car
- scissors
- colored markers
- masking tape
- 30 cm x 100 cm or 1 ft x 3 ft piece of corrugated cardboard
- props
- measuring tape

PROCEDURE

1 From the thin cardboard, cut out a skateboard shape slightly bigger than the toy car. Color and decorate it. Bend the back edge up slightly to make it look more realistic. Make a small loop of masking tape with the sticky side out and use it to attach the cardboard shape to the top of the toy car.

2 Prop one end of a piece of cardboard sheet 15 cm (6 in) off the floor to make a ramp. Set the skateboard at the top and release it so that it runs down and off the ramp. Do several trials and record how far the skateboard rolls in the table on the next page.

3 Raise the end of the cardboard ramp to 30 cm (12 in) and repeat the previous step. Record the distances in the table on the next page.

4 Calculate the average distance for each ramp height: Add up all the distances and divide by the number of trials.

HEIGHT OF RAMP	DISTANCE TRAVELED IN CM (IN)			
	TRIAL #1	TRIAL #2	TRIAL #3	AVERAGE
15 CM (6 IN)				
30 CM (12 IN)				

RESULTS

When you lift a weight off the ground, you store energy in it. In this case, the energy was stored in the skateboard and then released by letting the skateboard roll down the ramp. The higher you raised the weight, the more energy you stored. The more energy you stored, the farther the skateboard rolled. When the skateboard is at the top of the ramp and not moving, we say it has *potential* energy. When it is moving, we say the skateboard has *kinetic* energy.

You did more than one trial so that you could be sure the measurement was reliable. Calculating the average allowed you to compare results more easily.

FOR THE RECORD

There are two kinds of mechanical energy: potential and kinetic. They can be converted into each other.

TEST IT YOURSELF

What would happen if you started the skateboard halfway down the ramp?

A.D.I.S.N. SAYS:

Potential energy is all around us! Take a lake, for instance—it's a huge source of energy if it is stored behind a hydroelectric dam. When it flows downhill through the turbines, it converts the stored potential energy into electricity, which in turn can keep your devices charged—like me!

YOU'VE GOT THE
MOTION

. . . so get into the swing of things!

MATERIALS

- 90 mL or 3 fl oz plastic cup
- hole punch
- twist ties
- string
- ruler
- heavy books
- 20 pennies
- watch
- stopwatch

PROCEDURE

1. Punch two holes in the plastic cup just below the rim and across from each other. Secure one end of a twist tie in each hole. Bring the free ends of the twist ties side by side and twist them together for about 2 cm (1 in). This will form a "bucket handle" with the twisted part sticking straight up. Bend the tip over sideways to make a small hook.

2. Tie a small loop in one end of a 30 cm (12 in) length of string and a loop just large enough to fit over the ruler at the other end.

3. Repeat the previous step with a 60 cm (24 in) length of string.

4. Weigh the ruler down with heavy books so that about 10 cm (4 in) sticks out over the edge of a table.

5. Take the short string and hang it from the ruler. Put 10 pennies in the cup and hang the cup on the end of the string by the small hook. Pull the cup to the side, set the pendulum swinging, and time how long it takes to swing back and forth 10 times. Repeat two more times starting from different positions and record your results in the table on the next page.

6. Replace the short string with the long string and again measure the time it takes to swing back and forth 10 times. Repeat two more times starting from different positions and record your results.

7 Add 10 more pennies to the cup. Measure the time it takes to swing back and forth 10 times. Repeat two more times starting from different positions and record your results.

8 Switch back to the short string. Measure the time it takes to swing back and forth 10 times with the 20 pennies this time. Repeat two more times starting from different positions and record your results.

OBSERVATIONS

LENGTH	WEIGHT	TIME 1 (SEC)	TIME 2 (SEC)	TIME 3 (SEC)
30 CM (12 IN)	10 PENNIES			
60 CM (24 IN)	10 PENNIES			
30 CM (12 IN)	20 PENNIES			
60 CM (24 IN)	20 PENNIES			

RESULTS

A pendulum is an example of simple harmonic motion. This means that the weighted string swings back and forth in a regular pattern. In fact, the weighted string takes the same amount of time to swing back and forth (its period) no matter how far from the vertical you start the weight swinging. It just swings faster if the weight has to travel a greater distance. This is why pendulums are useful in building clocks. Gravity is the force driving this motion. It's also interesting that it does not matter how heavy the weight is—the period of the pendulum remains the same. You can change the period, however, by changing the length of the pendulum. A long pendulum takes longer to swing back and forth than a short pendulum.

FOR THE RECORD

A pendulum swings back and forth in a set amount of time no matter how far out the weight is pushed from the vertical. You can change the amount of time it takes to swing back and forth by changing the length of the pendulum.

TEST IT YOURSELF

Would the period of a pendulum be the same on the moon as on the earth? (Hint: What force causes a pendulum to swing back and forth?)

<3

A.D.I.S.N. SAYS:

The grandfather clock is a great example of a pendulum. A pendulum built upside down is the idea behind a metronome, a device musicians use to keep a steady rhythm or beat. That reminds me, I am a very talented musician in addition to being a brilliant notebook. Go ahead and open my music app. . . .

THE LAYERED LOOK

Density makes a fashion statement from top to bottom.

MATERIALS

- 4 clear 180 mL or 6 fl oz drinking glasses or jars
- measuring spoons
- 150 mL or 10 tbsp of 91% rubbing alcohol
- 120 mL or 8 tbsp of cooking oil
- 90 mL or 6 tbsp of water
- paper towels
- small plastic medicine droppers
- food coloring (optional)

PROCEDURE

1 Measure 30 mL (2 tbsp) of 91% rubbing alcohol into glass #1.

2 Measure 30 mL (2 tbsp) of cooking oil each into glass #2 and glass #3.

3 Measure 30 mL (2 tbsp) of water into glass #4.

4 Carefully pour 30 mL (2 tbsp) of cooking oil down the inside of glass #1 and glass #4 by directing the liquid with the tablespoon touching the inside of the glass. Wipe the tablespoon clean with a paper towel.

5 Run 30 mL (2 tbsp) of 91% rubbing alcohol down the inside of glass #2 in the same way.

6 Run 30 mL (2 tbsp) of water down the inside of glass #3 similarly.

7 If necessary, swirl once gently to smooth out the layers. Mixing too much will cause droplets to become suspended in the layers and make them cloudy. Record your results in the table on the next page.

8 Pour the contents of glass #3 into glass #4 carefully using the tablespoon as before. Allow the layers to settle for a minute. Wipe the tablespoon clean with a paper towel.

9 Now add 60 mL (4 tbsp) of 91% rubbing alcohol to glass #4 slowly, again using the tablespoon.

10 Fill the dropper with 91% rubbing alcohol by squeezing the bulb and placing the tip in the alcohol, then letting the bulb expand. Carefully submerge the dropper tip in glass #4 so that its tip is in the middle of the oil layer. Squeeze the bulb slowly and note what happens to the drops of alcohol that come out the tip. Wipe the dropper clean and rinse the inside with water. Now fill the dropper with water and repeat this step. Note what happens to the drops of water that come out the tip.

11 If desired, you can add food coloring to the alcohol and water. Because the oil is already yellow, you will get three very fashionable colored layers.

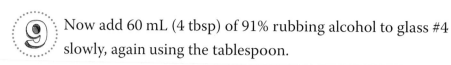

OBSERVATIONS

GLASS	ORDER OF ADDITION	TOP LAYER	BOTTOM LAYER
#1	OIL ADDED TO ALCOHOL		
#2	ALCOHOL ADDED TO OIL		
#3	WATER ADDED TO OIL		
#4	OIL ADDED TO WATER		

RESULTS

You have just stacked three layers of liquid according to a property called density. The density of a substance depends on how much material (mass) there is in a given space (volume). You can think of it as a measure of compactness. This means that if you took 30 mL (2 tbsp) of three different substances and weighed them, the lightest one would be the least dense and the heaviest one would be the most dense. In the case of the three liquids in your experiment, the liquid with the lowest density was on top and the one with the highest density was on the bottom.

FOR THE RECORD

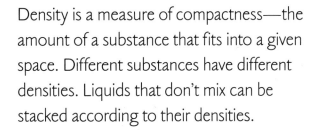

Density is a measure of compactness—the amount of a substance that fits into a given space. Different substances have different densities. Liquids that don't mix can be stacked according to their densities.

TEST IT YOURSELF

If you carefully added a piece of cork, a lump of candle wax, a plastic bread bag clip, and a metal paper clip to the three layers, would they float on top, float in the middle, or sink?

Which is heavier, a kilogram of bricks or a kilogram of feathers? (Careful . . . this is a trick question!)

A.D.I.S.N. SAYS:

When scientists study materials, they begin by determining their properties. Some properties just need to be observed, such as color, texture, and smell. Others need to be measured— like mass and volume. Density, or how much stuff is shoved into a space, is the ratio of these two things and is a fundamental property of everything. For instance, this room is way too crowded with all these NOV8 agents!

BLAST OFF!!

*Rockets are cool and all, but it's
the payload that counts.*

MATERIALS

- 15 cm x 15 cm or 6 in x 6 in square of aluminum foil
- 30 mm x 50 mm or $1\frac{3}{16}$ in x 2 in plastic film canister with plug-type cap
- satin-finish transparent tape
- cork, approximately 20 mm x 45 mm or $\frac{7}{8}$ in x 1 $\frac{3}{4}$ in
- black permanent marker
- effervescent antacid tablets
- 1 cup water
- modeling clay

PROCEDURE

THIS EXPERIMENT SHOULD BE PERFORMED OUTSIDE!

(Other small plastic bottles with snap-on lids will work, but the film canister described on p. 131 is the best. They can be readily ordered online.)

1 Roll up a 15 cm x 15 cm (6 in x 6 in) square of aluminum foil onto the film canister along one edge, with the canister's open end facing out. You will end up with a tube of aluminum foil with the film canister inside it at one end. Use a piece of satin-finish transparent tape to secure the seam on the section that holds the canister. It is important that no foil hangs over the edge of the canister so that the plug-type cap fits in cleanly.

2 Turn the roll over so the open end of the canister is flat down and drop the cork into the open end of the aluminum tube so it sits on top of the canister. Squeeze the foil evenly around the cork so the upper part of the tube is now narrower than the bottom. Pinch the excess foil above the cork into a point and shape the entire rocket so it is smooth and symmetrical.

3 Gently slip the canister out and secure the inside seam with a piece of satin-finish transparent tape. Slip the canister back in, with the bottom first and the open side out.

Draw features such as rocket engines, portholes, or riveted panels on the outside of the rocket with a permanent black marker.

 Your rocket is now ready for launch. Break an antacid tablet into quarters. Hold the rocket upside down and firmly around the canister end. Place one piece of "fuel" in the film canister "engine." Add about a tablespoon of water, seal the cap, and set the rocket on the ground. The tablet will begin bubbling right away, but don't rush. You have plenty of time to do all this, and it is important that the cap be closed properly. You can expect the rocket to blast off in about 30 seconds.

 It is now time to figure out how big a payload you can have and still achieve Earth orbit. Choose a convenient reference point like a tree or a fence about 3 m (10 ft) high. Push a small lump of modeling clay onto the tip of the rocket. Launch it and see how high it goes. If it flies a lot higher than the reference point, add more modeling clay and launch it again. If it does not go high enough, remove modeling clay and launch it again.

 Once you have determined the right size, mold the modeling clay into the shape of a satellite and launch it into orbit. Congratulations! You are now the director of a successful space program!

OBSERVATIONS AND RESULTS

Your rocket is an example of Newton's third law of motion: For every action, there is an equal and opposite reaction. The citric acid and sodium bicarbonate in the antacid tablet reacted to form carbon dioxide gas when they were dissolved in water. A lot of gas was generated in the film canister, so the pressure built up. Finally, the pressure was high enough to pop off the cap and let the contents come rushing out. To balance this sudden action, the film canister reacted by shooting up in the opposite direction, carrying the rocket with it.

There is only so much force, however, that a film canister "engine" can generate. If the weight is small, the rocket can go quite high. If it is heavy, the distance is much shorter. A real rocket needs to go at least 160 km (99 mi) high to achieve orbit around the earth. The reference point you chose for your rocket represented this height. You were able to figure out how big a "payload" you could "send into orbit" by conducting a series of launches where you varied the weight and observed the height. Rocket scientists are able to calculate this weight based on the size of the rocket engine, so they don't need to do multiple launches.

FOR THE RECORD

Rocket engines work by expelling gases at high pressure, causing the rocket to go in the opposite direction. The size of the payload depends on the power of the engine.

A.D.I.S.N. SAYS:

There are more than 1,100 active satellites circling Earth today—and none of them would be up there in the first place without rockets. They help us communicate, predict weather, and map the world.

TEST IT YOURSELF

Why are satellites usually carried inside a rocket and not just attached to the top?

SAND'S **HOT**, WATER'S **NOT**

Don't forget your flip-flops.

MATERIALS

- 45 mL or 3 tbsp of sand
- 60 mL or 4 tbsp of water
- 2 120–180 mL or 4–6 fl oz glass jars or drinking glasses
- shoe box
- desk lamp
- 2 air temperature thermometers

PROCEDURE

1. Add 45 mL (3 tbsp) of sand to one jar and 60 mL (4 tbsp) of water to the other.

2. Set the empty shoe box on a table and position the desk lamp right over it.

3. Carefully place the two jars in the shoebox and make sure they are both the same distance from the desk lamp.

4. Look at your thermometers and determine what unit the thermometers use to measure temperature. Circle the unit you are using in the table on the next page.

5. Put the thermometers into the glass jars and record the temperature that the thermometers read in the table on the next page.

6. Turn on the desk lamp and record the temperature of the water and sand every 2 minutes for 20 minutes.

7. Turn the lamp off and remove the thermometers from the glass jars. Feel the temperature of the water and sand with your fingers.

8. Calculate the temperature change by subtracting the temperature at 0 minutes from the temperature at 20 minutes.

OBSERVATIONS

TIME (MIN)	TEMPERATURE OF WATER (°F OR °C)	TEMPERATURE OF SAND (°F OR °C)
0		
2		
4		
6		
8		
10		
12		
14		
16		
18		
20		
TEMPERATURE CHANGE		

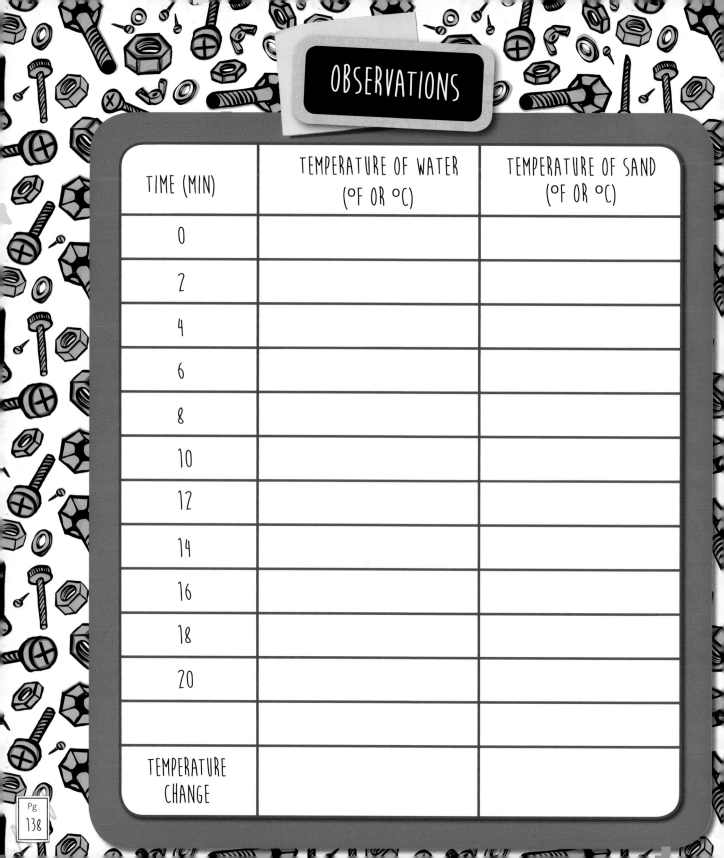

RESULTS

The rise in temperature for sand is greater than the rise for water. The sand feels warmer than the water. Under the same environmental conditions, sand heats up faster than water. This is one reason why the sand at the beach feels hot and the water feels cool in the summer.

The amount a substance heats up is related to its molecular structure and the amount of energy that it can store. The property you just examined is called the specific heat. Different substances have different specific heats. Water has the largest specific heat of any everyday substance we use. This means that it takes a lot of energy to heat up and increase its temperature. Sand is the opposite and has a low specific heat.

FOR THE RECORD

The ability to absorb heat and warm up is different for every substance. This property is called the specific heat.

A.D.I.S.N. SAYS:

Water helps regulate the temperature of Earth. The high specific heat means that water can absorb a lot of energy yet heat up slowly. It also cools down slowly, so that overall the temperature doesn't vary a lot. This is great for supporting life, and smart girls like Camryn.

TEST IT YOURSELF

What if you used flour instead of sand as your solid—would you see as large a temperature rise?

GETTING IN SHAPE: GEODESIC DOMES

Get to the point!

MATERIALS

- 16 thin inexpensive paper plates
- pencil
- protractor
- scissors
- ruler
- stapler

PROCEDURE

 1 Mark the exact center of a paper plate. Draw a line from this point to the edge of the plate. Using a protractor, draw two more lines to the edge of the plate at a 120° angle from the first line and from each other. Connect the three equally spaced marks at the edge of the plate with a pencil line. Cut along these outer lines to obtain a triangle shape.

 2 Using the triangle as a template, trace the triangle shape onto 15 plates. Fold the curved plate edges up along all the lines with the aid of a ruler. You should end up with triangle shapes with curved flaps folded up on all three sides.

 3 Line up two straight edges and staple the flaps of two plates together in two places. Continue stapling five plates together side by side till you have formed a floppy pentagon.

 MAKE SURE AN ADULT IS AROUND TO HELP FOR STEPS #3, 4 +5!

4 Staple five more plates to the free edges of the pentagon so it takes on a star shape.

 5 Staple the remaining five plates between each of the star points along both sides. The overall structure will become more rigid and basketlike. Set the structure on a table and examine it.

 6 If desired, you can trim the flaps to emphasize the geodesic structure, but it is not necessary for this experiment.

Every corner (vertex) is the center of what geometric shape?

How many vertices are there? How many edges? How many faces?

Press gently on the top vertex. Note how the structure flexes.

Press gently in the middle of a top triangle. Note how the structure flexes.

RESULTS

A geodesic dome is a curved form made up of repeating geometric shapes. The overall structure is usually part of a sphere while the geometric shape is most often a triangle. You are basically trying to make a round structure using only straight lines.

For building structures, a sphere or dome is a practical form, because it encloses the most amount of space with the least amount of surface area. This means it takes less material to construct it. Using triangles as a framework gives the structure strength because of the way the weight is spread out evenly. This is what you were testing when you pushed on different parts of the structure. An added advantage is that you don't need a separate framework to hold it up—the structure itself is the framework. There is no need for pillars or support beams.

The shape you made is actually part of an icosahedron. This is a 20-sided solid form made up of only triangles. You would have to add 5 more paper plate triangles to the bottom of your structure to turn it into one. Despite all the straight lines, the icosahedron is surprisingly ball shaped and so a good place to start when constructing a geodesic dome.

FOR THE RECORD

A geodesic dome is a round structure made up of repeating geometric shapes. The design is exceptionally strong, which allows the use of lightweight construction materials.

TEST IT YOURSELF

The icosahedron is a 20-sided solid shape made up of triangles. What is the smallest number of triangles you can use to make a solid form? (Hint: It is called a tetrahedron.)

A.D.I.S.N. SAYS:

In principle, geodesic domes can be enormous. Some scientists and engineers have imagined ones big enough to enclose entire cities. A structure like that could be very useful, especially on the moon! (A place I will one day travel to, to be the first ever Advanced Digital Intelligence Spy Notebook in Space!)

SCIENTIFIC OBSERVATIONS

ACKNOWLEDGMENTS

SPECIAL THANKS TO THESE SECRET AGENTS:

Michael Anderson

Alessandra Bellissimo

Juli Boylan

Lisa Foster

Paula Garcia

Anne Gates

Leah George

Sam Khare

Minna Kim

Isaac Larian

Amritz Lay

Ilse Lopez

Alexandra Mack

Corinne Mescher

Sadaf Cohen Muncy

Tamara Rothenberg

Danica Scaglione

Jeff Vinokur

Andy Yeatman

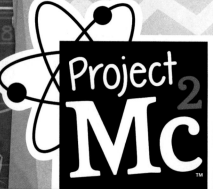
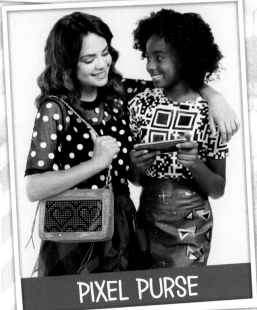